Click-clack, click-clack . . .

From morning till night, our shoes carry us through the world–through the streets, through the parks, and into our homes. But what happens to our shoes when we take them off?

"Nothing," say those who don't believe in soles.

"Shhhh! It's a secret!" say others, who believe that our shoes lead a wonderful life of their own.

No one knows for sure. What if, in every one of our shoes, a real little person was hiding, a strange creature, an elf, a Tom Thumb, who cautiously stuck his nose out as soon as we turned our backs? But then, as soon as someone came near, poof, he disappeared. That's why we can never see the little shoe people . . . except in this book. A paintbrush and a pencil have successfully slipped into this small secret world, and here's the incredible story they have to tell.

Copyright © 2006 by NordSüd Verlag AG, Gossau Zürich, Switzerland
First published in Switzerland under the title *Fräulein Bixel und Herr Glück*
English translation copyright © 2006 by North-South Books Inc., New York

All rights reserved. No part of this book may be reproduced or utilized in any
form or by any means, electronic or mechanical, including photocopying,
recording, or any information storage and retrieval system, without permission
in writing from the publisher.

First published in the United States, Great Britain, Canada, Australia,
and New Zealand in 2006 by North-South Books, an imprint of
NordSüd Verlag AG, Gossau Zürich, Switzerland.
Distributed in the United States by North-South Books Inc., New York.

Library of Congress Cataloging-in-Publication Data is available.
A CIP catalogue record for this book is available from The British Library.

ISBN-13: 978-0-7358-2067-8 / ISBN-10: 0-7358-2067-8  (trade edition)
10 9 8 7 6 5 4 3 2 1

Printed in Belgium

Susanne Vettiger · Maria Blazejovsky

# *Mr. Right Is Missing!*

Translated by Sibylle Kazeroid

North-South Books
New York / London

Every morning when Miss Left woke up, she would turn to her right. "Good morning, Mr. Right," she'd say, and then she'd ask, "did you sleep well?" This was how Miss Left had started her day for almost nine years. It was always the same–rain or shine, winter or summer, Tuesdays or Sundays.

And for almost nine years Mr. Right had answered, "Good morning, Miss Left. I slept very well, thank you." Then he would smile and turn to the left–toward Miss Left.

Miss Left and Mr. Right were very fond of each other. Even though they'd known each other for years, they didn't call each other by their first names, as most friends do. Instead, they addressed each other as "Miss" and "Mr." They considered themselves very proper. You see, Miss Left and Mr. Right lived in the opera house, where everything was very elegant and very distinguished.

Whenever they appeared onstage, Miss Left was always on the left and Mr. Right was always on the right. That's because Miss Left and Mr. Right were a pair of shoes! One of 365 pairs of shoes in the opera house.

Until, that is, one fateful morning . . .

"Good morning, Mr. Right. Did you sleep well?"

For the first time in almost nine years, Mr. Right didn't answer. In fact he couldn't, because the spot to the right of Miss Left was empty.

"Mr. Right is missing!" she gasped.

"What was that noise?" Miss Left was suddenly wide awake. The whole opera house jerked and quaked, sparked and sawed and shrieked.

Miss Left was most confused. She had seen lots of operas. Her favorites were *The Magic Flute*, *Aida*, and *La Bohème*. She also liked ballet—especially *The Nutcracker*. She knew that building scenery for the opera or the ballet always made quite a racket, but she'd never heard anything quite like what she heard this morning.

"Mr. Right, where are you?" called Miss Left desperately.

"Oh, he'll come back soon enough. What's a right shoe going to do all by himself?" said the pair next to her.

"Maybe he had a bad dream and fell off the shelf. That happened to me once," chuckled someone else, and the pointy shoes with the high heels nodded, grinning. Miss Left wasn't amused at all. "That's very mean of you. What if something bad happened to him?" she said.

"What if he's outside? We've seen what it's like there," said the rain boots. They were the only shoes that ever got to go outside. "Streets full of galoshes with holes and old worn-out sneakers!"

Miss Left was so upset she could hardly breathe. "Mr. Right is not an old worn-out sneaker!" she said indignantly. But now she was really worried about Mr. Right.

"Well, my dears," said a friendly human voice. "Which ones should I take next? Oh, I know, this elegant high-heeled red one and that black flat, those will do nicely. And there's the one made from real cowhide. Perfect!" The friendly human voice belonged to Wendy. She was in charge of the 365 pairs of shoes in the opera house. Wendy repaired, glued, dyed, and cleaned them and was so nice to them; it was as if they were her children. Sometimes she even named them.

For example, there was Mr. and Mrs. Zack, Max and Moritz, Lilly and Lisa, and Miss Left and Mr. Right. Sometimes Wendy even talked to her shoes, but today she didn't have time. She grabbed one red, one black, and one yellow shoe and dashed off. Each time she took only one shoe from each pair and left the other behind.

She kept coming back, all day long. Sometimes she'd take the left shoe, sometimes the right. And the next day it continued. After three days she still hadn't stopped. Soon Miss Left was surrounded by shoes who felt as lonely and abandoned as she did. "It's terrible to be separated. We feel like . . . like . . . a car without wheels. Or Easter without eggs. Or a birthday cake without candles."

Miss Left felt more like Miss Left Behind!

All the shoes were worried. Those that disappeared still hadn't come back. What had Wendy done with them?

"Maybe she's cutting off all the heels!" said a black patent leather shoe. "Maybe she sold them, and we'll never be paired up again."

"This isn't right! We have to do something," said Miss Left in despair. But what could they do? They were only shoes. Single shoes. Only the rain boots were still a pair. "She's completely ignoring us," they moaned, "even though it's raining outside."

"Oh, Mr. Right," sniffled Miss Left sadly. And from the long shelves, many voices sighed with her.

At last, Wendy came into the wardrobe where the shoes
were carefully arranged.

"Not one pair left," she said proudly, not noticing the rain boots.
"I'm finished!"

She shouted so loudly that Ernest the cat, who cared only
about catnip and nice bowls of milk, jumped in the air with fright.

"Come here," said Wendy to the cat. "I have something to
show you."

The door to the opera workshop was wide open. In the middle was a centipede as big as a dinosaur, made out of wood. The centipede had 364 feet, and on each foot was a real shoe.

"So, what do you think of that?" whispered Wendy in Ernest's ear. "Tonight is the premiere. *King Centipede and the Princess.* It's an opera for children. We'll all go too—we have front row seats."

The audience loved the opera, which was about a king
with hundreds of feet who rescues a beautiful princess.

The high point of the evening was when the king tap-danced on the stage wearing all 364 shoes.

After the premiere there was a party. But not for Miss Left, Mr. Right, and their friends. After the very last performance, when all the pairs of shoes were finally reunited, they celebrated. They danced all night long. Everyone danced with each other, and the shoes got all mixed up. But in the morning they were back on the shelves again, red next to red, black next to black, and Miss Left next to Mr. Right. When he woke up, Mr. Right turned shyly to Miss Left, "By the way, my name is Roland."

"I'm Annabelle," she said softly. But that was their secret. To Wendy and the other shoes they would always be Miss Left and Mr. Right.